Welcome to
The Giggle Club

The Giggle Club is a collection of picture books made to put a giggle into early reading. There are funny stories about a contrary mouse, a dancing fox, a turtle with a trumpet, a pig with a ball, a hungry monster, a laughing lobster, an elephant who sneezes away the jungle and lots more! Each of these characters is a member of **The Giggle Club**, but anyone can join: just pick up a **Giggle Club** book, read it and get giggling!

Turn to the checklist on the inside back cover and tick off the Giggle Club books you have read.

EE HEE!

HA HA!

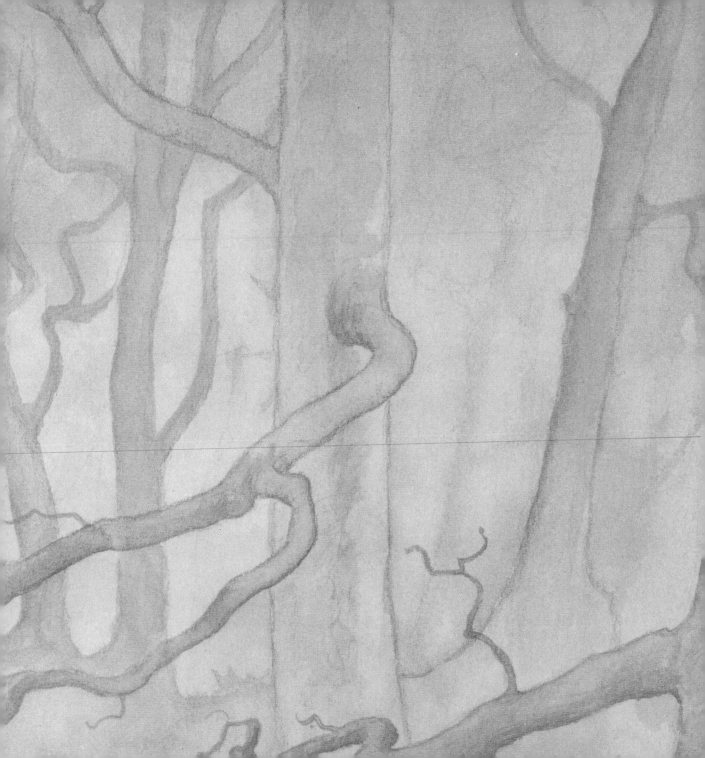

For Trisha

First published 1996 by Walker Books Ltd
87 Vauxhall Walk, London SE11 5HJ

This edition published 1997

4 6 8 10 9 7 5 3

© 1996 Tony Kerins

This book has been typeset in Sabon.

Printed in Hong Kong

British Library Cataloguing in Publication Data
A catalogue record for this book is available
from the British Library.

ISBN 0-7445-5283-4

THE
BRAVE
ONES

TONY KERINS

WALKER BOOKS
AND SUBSIDIARIES
LONDON • BOSTON • SYDNEY

We are the Brave Ones, marching
home through the woods.
Polly and Jim. Big Eric.
Barker the dog. Birdy the bird.
But not Little Clancy.
Little Clancy is safe
back at home.

Wooo! Wooo!
We aren't afraid of the
wind in the woods. We are
the Brave Ones! Polly and Jim,
Big Eric, Barker and Birdy.
But not Little Clancy.
Little Clancy is safe
back at home.

Rustle! Rustle!

We aren't afraid
of the leaves in the trees.
We are the Brave Ones!
Polly and Jim, Big Eric,
Barker and Birdy.
But not Little Clancy.
Little Clancy is safe
back at home.

Crack! Crack!

We aren't afraid of the twigs and the branches. We are the Brave Ones! Polly and Jim, Big Eric, Barker and Birdy. But not Little Clancy. Little Clancy is safe back at home...

And so we march on. All the way back. We are the Brave Ones!

Here we all are safe back at home.
Polly and Jim. Big Eric. Barker
the dog. Birdy the bird. But not
Little Clancy. Where *is* Little Clancy?

Outside it is dark
with wild windy sounds.
Inside it is cosy and
quiet. We are glad we are
home from the woods.

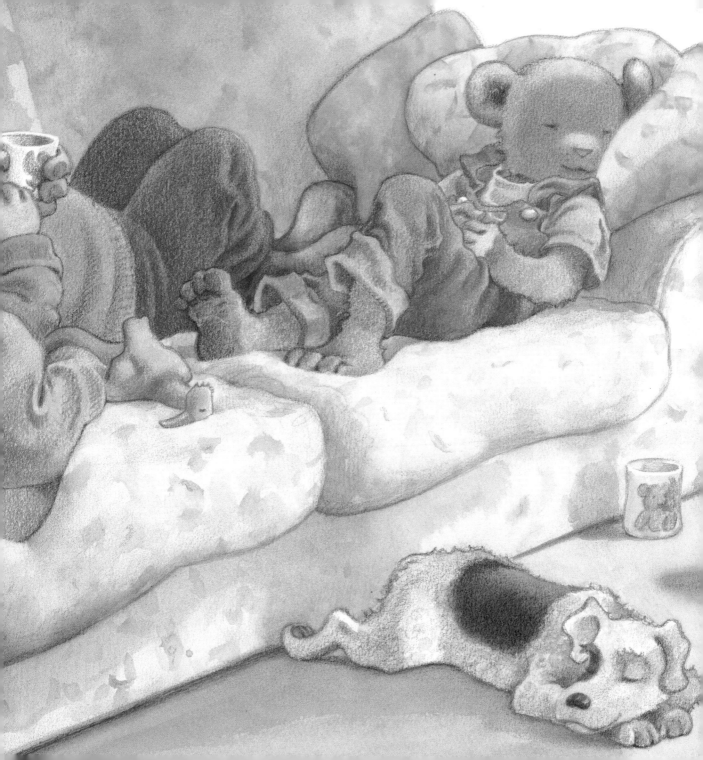

Who made that terrible noise?
Who gave us all a terrible fright?
LITTLE CLANCY!
"Welcome home, Brave Ones!"
says Little Clancy.